THE ONLY BOY IN
Ballet Class

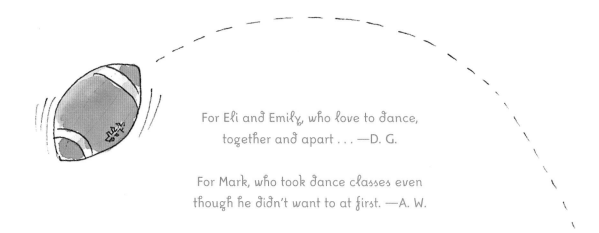

For Eli and Emily, who love to dance,
together and apart . . . —D. G.

For Mark, who took dance classes even
though he didn't want to at first. —A. W.

First Edition
11 10 09 08 07   5 4 3 2 1

Published by
Gibbs Smith, Publisher
P.O. Box 667
Layton, Utah 84041

Orders: 1.800.835.4993
www.gibbs-smith.com

Designed by Sheryl Dickert Smith
Printed and bound in China
Library of Congress Cataloging-in-Publication Data

Gruska, Denise Eliana.
  The only boy in ballet class / Denise Eliana Gruska ; illustrations by Amy Wummer. — 1st ed.
     p. cm.
  Summary: Tucker Dohr loves ballet but is constantly teased by football players his age for being a sissy, however
they see him in a whole new light when circumstances place him in a position to help them win the football
championship.
  ISBN-13: 978-1-4236-0220-0
  ISBN-10: 1-4236-0220-X
  [1. Ballet dancing—Fiction. 2. Football—Fiction. 3. Teasing—Fiction.] I. Wummer, Amy, ill. II. Title.

PZ7.G934125On 2007
[E]—dc22
                    2006102584

THE ONLY BOY IN
Ballet Class

Written by
DENISE GRUSKA

with Illustrations by
Amy Wummer

Gibbs Smith, Publisher
TO ENRICH AND INSPIRE HUMANKIND
Salt Lake City | Charleston | Santa Fe | Santa Barbara

Tucker Dohr loves to dance. But it's a long time until ballet class, so when he wakes up in the morning, that's when the waiting begins.

First, he has to leap over Marbles,
the cat, who likes to be in everybody's way.

Then he has to spin past his tricky,
tricky twin sisters, Blanche and Edie, who
are always plotting.

After that he has to go
way up on tiptoe past his
mom and her cup of coffee.
Tucker tries not to make
too much noise until after
the coffee's all gone. Twice.

Then he might have to
chassé or *pas de bourrée* to
school.

Later when Tucker sits at his desk and listens to how Magellan proved the roundness of the world, his feet have to keep moving.

The other kids think he's weird, but he can't help it. It feels right to him. Like breathing.

And even though he can move double fast, and jump triple tall, he's always the last one to be picked for softball. And basketball. And volleyball.

He tries to pretend that he doesn't care. He reminds himself that he'd rather dance anyway.

(But sometimes he has to cry about it at night when he's alone.)

When school is finally, finally over, Tucker walks three blocks and turns left where he passes the boys going to football practice with their cleats hanging over their shoulders.

Tucker walks the other way with his dance bag hanging over his shoulder. That's when he hears it. "Yo, Tippy-Toe Boy! Where's your tutu? Dancing is for girls!"

Tucker wants to tell them that dancing can be for anyone, even them, but he just keeps his eyes low and his feet moving instead.

As soon as Tucker pushes open the door to Madame Clara's Dance Studio, it happens. He stands a little taller.

When he takes off his shoes and pulls on his very worn-out ballet slippers, he jumps even higher than usual. It feels like flying. He likes to carve the air with the other dancers.

Even though Tucker is the only boy in ballet class, no one teases him here. And before he can double blink, it's time to go home.

He passes the boys who play football going the other way. "Check you later, Ballerina Boy!"

At home, Tucker sets the table for his mom. Sometimes he does it in *relevé* and balances a plate on his head for practice. Mostly, Blanche and Edie try to trip him up.

Every Tuesday, Uncle Frank comes over for dinner.

When Tucker brings the dessert bowls to the table with a *rond de jambe*,
Uncle Frank shakes his head, looks at Tucker's mother, and says, "You ought
to put that boy in football."

Sometimes that bothers Tucker, so he finds an excuse to *cabriole* over to his mom, like he has to bring her twenty-seven extra napkins for Blanche and Edie.

He leans in low and whispers in her ear, "Mom, do you like that I love to dance?" She holds his face close so that he can see the smile behind her eyes and says, "I don't *like* that you love to dance. I *love* that you love to dance!"

That's when Uncle Frank usually looks at his watch.

And things went on just like that until one Sunday afternoon when Tucker had a dance recital. He was so excited about it, he was touching the ground even less than usual.

He decided to invite his whole family, even Uncle Frank. Maybe then he could show his uncle how dancing was exactly right for him, Tucker Dohr.

When they walked past the football field on the way to the recital, Tucker held his breath, but luckily the boys who play football were too busy arguing with each other to even notice him.

Now the really good thing about being the only boy in ballet class is that you usually almost always get a great part, which means that you usually almost always get to be The Prince.

When Tucker took a bow after the recital, he could see that his mom was very proud. Even his sisters stopped plotting and stood up to clap.

But Uncle Frank, who looked at his watch even more than usual, just shook his head, and said a little too loudly, "I'm telling ya, you ought to put that boy in football."

This time, when they walked back to go home, the boys who play football all turned to look at Tucker. All at once, they started yelling at him.

He tried to pretend they were talking to someone else. He tried to get his mom, his sisters, and his uncle to walk faster, but the boys who play football were racing towards him.

Tucker started to run, but one of the boys grabbed him by the back of his shirt and spun him around. Tucker held his breath in and his fists up high when the boy said, "Hey, Twinkle Toes, wanna play football?"

Tucker was so surprised, he forgot to answer the question.

The kid stepped closer. "They won't let us finish the game unless we have eleven players on the field. Or we forfeit. And it's a championship. All you have to do is stand there."

Tucker started shaking his head no, when a voice boomed out over his shoulder. "He'd love to." Tucker knew who it was. He didn't even have to turn around.

They put a way too big uniform on Tucker, and before he could even the push the bowl of the helmet off his forehead to see, he was standing on a football field. They put Tucker behind the quarterback. *Way* behind the quarterback, and *way* out of the way. In a split instant, the ball was snapped.

The quarterback caught it and started moving
back to throw the ball when two boys on the other
team slammed into him, hard. The ball popped out of
the quarterback's hands, up into the air, and dropped
straight into Tucker's arms. And there it stayed.

There was a moment where everyone was too stunned to move.

Then Uncle Frank's voice boomed out, "Run!" Tucker looked at all the boys who wanted to mow him over. He decided that for once, Uncle Frank might be right. So Tucker ran!

And suddenly, the whole other team was chasing him. Just when two kids were about to drag him down hard, Tucker Dohr did something.

He *pirouetted* past the first kid, and he got away. Then he *jetéd* past the second one, and he got away. From then on, he knew exactly what to do. He *sautéd* and *assembléd* and *chaînéd* around every growling kid until they had to yell "Stop!" because he was almost to the street. And just like that, they won the game.

In the point of a toe, he was on the shoulders of every boy who had ever made fun of him, and they were carrying him across the field chanting, "Tuck-er! Tuck-er! Tuck-er!" Even Uncle Frank was dancing.

The day after that, when Tucker went to Madame Clara's, there was a pile of sneakers outside the door he had never seen before. He peered into the class. There they were—the boys who play football. Well, most of them. And they were doing . . . *pliés*. Well, sort of.

Madame Clara's School of Dance

Tucker stepped in. They all started shouting at once. "Hey, Tucker, teach us the part where you jump over the guy." "And that move you make when you're here and then suddenly you're over there." Tucker smiled as big as an *arabesque,* and leapt into the air.

He may no longer have been the only boy in ballet class, but he was positively the happiest.

Ballet Terms

in order of appearance

Chassé (*sha-SAY*): when you "chase," one foot following the other

Pas de bourrée (*PAH de boo-RAY*): when you move quickly with small, linked steps

Relevé (*reh-leh-VAY*): when you go up on tiptoe

Rond de jambe (*RON de JAHMB*): when you circle your leg around, on the ground, or in the air

Cabriole (*ka-bree-OLE*): when you jump and clap your legs together and apart in the air

Pirouette (*peer-WET*): when you spin like a top on one leg

Jeté (*juh-TAY*): when you leap forward from one foot to the other

Sauté (*soh-TAY*): when you jump straight up in the air

Assemblé (*a-sahm-BLAY*): when you leap in the air, bring your feet together, and land a ways away

Chaîné (*sheh-NAY*): when you link turns together

Plié (*plee-AY*): when you bend your knees

Arabesque (*ar-a-BESK*): when you stand on one leg with the other leg stretched out in the air behind you